READING

RECOVERY

The TREE HOUSE DETECTIVE CLUB

Written by Elizabeth Bolton
Illustrated by S.D. Schindler

Troll Associates

Library of Congress Cataloging in Publication Data

Bolton, Elizabeth.
    The Tree House Detective Club.

    Summary: The Walnut Street Detectives prove their worth
to the neighborhood when they help foil a robbery.
    1. Children's stories, American. [1. Mystery and
detective stories] I. Schindler, S. D., ill. II. Title.
PZ7.B63597Tr   1985   [Fic]   84-8762
ISBN 0-8167-0404-X (lib. bdg.)
ISBN 0-8167-0405-8 (pbk.)

The TREE HOUSE DETECTIVE CLUB

"We've got a problem," I said.

Jay Bradley looked at me. "The Careys?"
he asked.

I nodded.

Jay whistled. "Wow," he said. "That's a
real problem."

"I don't see why the Careys are a
problem," said Meg. "They're nice."

Stinky Morgan groaned. Jenny Miller rolled her eyes. We were all up in my tree house. The Walnut Street Detective Club was in session.

"The Careys *are* nice," I said patiently.
"But they say we make too much noise. They
don't like us watching them through our
spyglass. And they *don't* like our tree house!"

7

"Why not? I think it's great," said Jenny.
She was hanging upside down from a branch.
"Besides, it's been here for a year. How come
they don't like it now?"

"They used to go to work. Now they're retired. So they're home and they can see and hear us."

"This is serious," said Jay.

"I'll say it is," I said, and I knocked on the tree-house floor. "The Walnut Street Detective Club will come to order. Mr. Carey told my dad this tree house is an awful old wreck."

"It is not an old wreck!" said Stinky. He's called Stinky because he's always stepping on stinkweed plants in the woods. "My dad's a builder. He says this tree house is as solid as a rock!"

"I don't think that's what Mr. Carey means," Meg said.

We looked around. The tree house did look pretty bad. There were two banana peels and a couple of old apple cores on the floor. There was an old T-shirt Stinky had hung up two months ago for a pirate flag. Maybe the Carey's didn't like living next door to pirates.

"Detective hide-outs aren't supposed to be in other peoples backyards. That's what Mr. Carey says," I told them. "Mr. Carey says he's sorry, but the tree house has to come down."

"That's terrible!" said Meg.

"We've got to find a way to fight back!" Jenny said.

"We have to find a way to show him a tree house isn't bad," I said. "We have to prove detectives are good neighbors."

"I can't believe this," Meg said. "Mrs. Carey always gives us cookies. When we solved the case of the missing cookies, Mr. Carey said he was proud of us."

We formed the Walnut Street Detective Club to solve that mystery. The thief turned out to be my beagle dog, Wallace. He could reach the Carey's kitchen windowsill when he stood on his hind legs. "That was months ago," I said. "We haven't had a case since."

"There's never any trouble in this neighborhood," Jay sighed.

"We'd better all go home and think," I said at last. "Take your junk with you. And *don't* yell or cut through the Carey's yard!"

I didn't feel like eating dinner that night. I didn't feel like talking either.

"What's the matter, Mike? Cat got your tongue?" Dad asked.

"I'm thinking about the tree house," I said gloomily.

"Oh," Dad nodded. "You'd better eat anyway. Keep your strength up. You'll need it if we're going to save the tree house."

That sounded hopeful. I decided I could eat some dessert after all.

All that was on Tuesday. On Wednesday Jay said, "Maybe if the tree house looked better the Careys wouldn't think it's an old wreck." So that afternoon we cleaned house. We took down the pirate flag. We swept the floor. We made sure nothing fell down into the Carey's yard.

18

19

On Wednesday night, I asked Dad if we were going to have to take the tree house down. He said, "I don't know yet."

On Thursday after dinner, Stinky's dad came over. He checked the ladder steps. He checked the railing and the roof and the door. "Everything's safe and solid," he said. "This is not a wreck."

On Saturday we had a special meeting of the Walnut Street Detective Club. Wallace wanted to come, too. He sat at the bottom of the ladder and howled.

"For goodness sake, Mike, get him away from here!" said Meg. "The Careys will have fits!"

I wouldn't blame the Careys if they did. For a little dog, Wallace sure can sound like a howling monster. After I dragged him into the house, we sat around our neat, clean tree house staring at each other. We tried not to make a sound.

Jay gave a sigh. "We're doing everything we can think of to be good neighbors. We'll just have to hope the Careys agree."

From the tree house we could see my dad. He was out on the side lawn fussing with his roses. Mr. Carey came over to him. We hung over the railing, trying to listen.

"The week's up tomorrow," Mr. Carey said.

"Yup," said Dad. He was real cool. He just went on pruning the roses.

Mr. Carey looked sad. "I like you folks, Hank. And I like Mike a lot. But I absolutely do not like that tree house. What's more, it's got no business being there."

Dad turned to face him. He was still smiling. His voice sounded nice. But he said, "Since when don't kids have a right to play in their own yard, Lewis?"

"That tree hangs over into my yard,
Hank," Mr. Carey said. "I just plain don't
want all the neighborhood kids hanging over
into my yard, too. Who knows what mischief
or trouble they could get in? I'm sorry, but if
that tree house doesn't come down tomorrow,
I'll see you in court."

I remember the cake Mrs. Carey had
baked for my birthday last year. It made me
feel sad. Mom looked like she felt the same
way. "Anyway, the Careys will be away till
Friday," she said. "That's four days we won't
have to worry about the tree house!"

On Sunday the tree house didn't come down. But we stayed away from it. Our parents made us.

On Monday morning I saw Mr. and Mrs. Carey putting suitcases into their car. "They're going to visit their married daughter," Mom said. "It's their grandson's birthday."

I still worried. So did Jay. So did Meg
and Stinky and Jenny. But there wasn't
anything else we could do. Up in our club we
only whispered, even though the Careys
weren't there to hear. We didn't even *feel*
like making noise. That was because Dad got
a notice in the mail. It said he had to go to
court about the tree house next Monday
night.

On Thursday afternoon the Walnut Street
Detective Club met in the tree house for the
last time. Mom didn't want us up there. But
Mom wasn't home. And the Careys were still
away. So we all figured it was safe.

There was a lump in my throat. I didn't want the other kids to know. I picked up the spyglass and pretended to be looking through it.

All of a sudden the skin on my neck started to prickle. There was a truck parked in front of the Carey's house. There were two men on the porch. They were carrying a TV set.

Jay was looking over my shoulder. "Hey," he said, "the Careys must be getting a new TV."

"Why are the men carrying the TV *away* from the house?" Jenny asked. Suddenly, everybody got very quiet.

The men put the TV in the truck. They went back into the house. They came out carrying Mr. Carey's stereo.

"A robbery," Meg said. And the Walnut Street Detectives were the only ones seeing it happen!

"We mustn't scare them off," Jay whispered.

"We mustn't get them mad," Stinky added. "We can't let them see us!"

"We've got to call the police," Jenny said.

I was looking at my house. My bedroom window opened onto our roof, and that came right out to our tree house. "I think I can climb from the tree onto the roof," I whispered.

"Just don't let anybody see you," warned Jay.

I was glad the tree leaves were thick enough to hide me. I was just hoping Wallace wouldn't bark.

Meg was looking through the spyglass. "I can see the truck's license plate," she whispered. "It's EXK-226. Tell the police."

I had to be careful not to make any noise.
Jenny and Stinky held the tree branch steady.
"Stay in the tree house till I call you,"
I whispered. I inched along the branch until
my feet touched the roof. Then I slid off
and crouched down. The tree leaves hid me.
I climbed over to my window and crawled
inside.

Wallace was in there. He must have known this was important. His tail wagged like crazy, but he didn't make a sound. I tiptoed to the telephone with Wallace behind me. I asked the operator to get me the police.

Officer Simmons answered. That was good. He knew me from Little League. I said, "This is Mike Winters. I live at 461 Walnut Street, and there are burglars breaking in next door."

After that things happened fast. I heard
Officer Simmons pushing buzzers and
speaking into a microphone. Then he came
back on the phone and spoke to me. "Why are
you sure they're robbers, Mike?" he asked.

"The Careys are away. These men came in a strange truck. The license is EXK-226. The Walnut Street Detectives have been watching from our tree house. Please, Officer Simmons, hurry before the thieves get away!"

"Relax, partner," Officer Simmons said. "There's a squad car on the way now." Suddenly, I could hear a police siren wailing.

"Gee, thanks, Officer Simmons. Good-bye," I said quickly.

"Mike! Stay in your house till it's all over," Officer Simmons said sharply. "That's an order, partner. Understand?"

"Yes, sir." I put the phone down slowly. At least he called me partner, I thought. But it was awful to miss all the excitement.

Wallace and I watched from the window.
We could see the other detectives watching
from the tree house. None of us made a
sound. Two police cars blocked the truck.
A police officer was standing talking on his
radio. Two more officers were marching the
robbers down the porch steps.

All at once a blue car came around the corner. Mr. and Mrs. Carey jumped out. They talked to the police. They looked at the things the officers carried back from the truck. After the police drove the robbers away, they went inside their house.

I went back to the tree house. Jay and Meg and Jenny and Stinky were waiting for me. "We stayed here like you told us to," Jay said. "Gosh, it was hard!"

I took a deep breath. "I stayed in the house like Officer Simmons told *me* to. And it sure *was* hard!"

"The Walnut Street Detective Club has solved a big case at last," Meg said. "I'll bet the Careys will be glad now that we were up here."

"They don't even know about it," Stinky said sadly.

"Maybe we could tell them," said Jenny.

Somehow that didn't seem right. Anyway, first we had to tell our moms and dads.

"You did exactly right. I'm proud of you," Dad told me.

"I'm glad you stayed in the house as you were told to," said Mom. She gave me an extra big dish of ice cream for dessert that evening.

We were still at the dinner table when the telephone rang. Dad answered it. He came back looking serious. "Mr. Carey wants to see all the Walnut Street Detectives in the tree house in fifteen minutes."

I didn't know what to expect—neither did Jay or Meg or Jenny or Stinky. We quickly swept the tree house floor. We hid the spyglass. Then we heard footsteps on the ladder. A head appeared in the doorway—*two* heads! Both Mr. and Mrs. Carey had come. My insides did flip-flops.

Mr. and Mrs. Carey came inside. The Walnut Street Detectives stood up. We all looked at each other. Mr. Carey cleared his throat. "I came to apologize," he said. "I was wrong. The Walnut Street Detectives *are* good neighbors."

"The tree house doesn't have to come down?" asked Meg.

Mr. Carey's eyes twinkled. "The tree house doesn't have to come down. In fact—" He shook out a bundle of cloth. "Mrs. Carey and I have been making this ever since the police left. We noticed you didn't have a flag flying any more."

"W.S.D.C." read the new flag in cheerful orange and green. Those letters stood for the Walnut Street Detective Club!

"I don't even mind the spyglass anymore," Mr. Carey said. "It sure comes in handy. And this really is a fine tree house. But won't you come back to our house for lemonade and cookies?"

We were glad to. But first we hung up our great new flag. Then we voted Mr. and Mrs. Carey honorary members. The Walnut Street Detective Club was here to stay!